10 Draw the rest of the monkey.

You know how to draw a head!

Another arm

Draw an arm and a hand with five fingers.

Belly button

Squiggly tummy fur

Add squiggles here and there for fur.

Two legs

Two feet with five toes each

To download a free audio version of this story,

visit the "Books and More" page at

www.fivelittlemonkeys.com

Access code:

FIVE Little MONKEYS
jumping on the bed

Retold and Illustrated by
Eileen Christelow

CLARION BOOKS

Houghton Mifflin Harcourt ★ Boston New York

For

Heather   Morgan

Joni

Grady   Stefan

Clarion Books
215 Park Avenue South
New York, New York 10003

Clarion Books is an imprint of Houghton Mifflin Harcourt Publishing Company.

www.hmhco.com

Library of Congress Cataloging-in-Publication Data

Christelow, Eileen, author, illustrator.
Five little monkeys jumping on the bed / retold and illustrated by Eileen Christelow.—25th anniversary edition.
pages cm
Summary: A counting book in which one by one the little monkeys jump on the bed only to fall off and bump their heads.
ISBN 978-0-544-28329-9 (hardback)
1. Nursery rhymes. 2. Children's poetry. [1. Nursery rhymes. 2. Monkeys—Poetry. 3. Counting.] I. Title.

PZ8.3.C456Fi 2014
398.8—dc23

2014007587

Manufactured in China
SCP 10 9 8 7 6 5 4 3 2 1
4500478456

It was bedtime. So five little monkeys took a bath.

Five little monkeys put on their pajamas.

Five little monkeys brushed their teeth.

Five little monkeys said good night to their mama.

Then…five little monkeys jumped on the bed!

One fell off and bumped his head.

The mama called the doctor. The doctor said,

"No more monkeys jumping on the bed!"

So four little monkeys...

…jumped on the bed.

14

One fell off and bumped his head.

The mama called the doctor.

The doctor said,

"No more monkeys jumping on the bed!"

17

So three little monkeys jumped on the bed.

One fell off and bumped her head.

The mama called the doctor.

The doctor said,

"No more monkeys jumping on the bed!"

So two little monkeys jumped on the bed.

One fell off and bumped his head.

The mama called the doctor.

The doctor said,

"No more monkeys jumping on the bed!"

So one little monkey jumped on the bed.

She fell off and bumped her head.

The mama called the doctor.

The doctor said,

"NO MORE MONKEYS JUMPING ON THE BED!"

So five little monkeys fell fast asleep.

"Thank goodness!" said the mama.

"Now I can go to bed!"

Five Little Monkeys Jumping on the Bed

Traditional

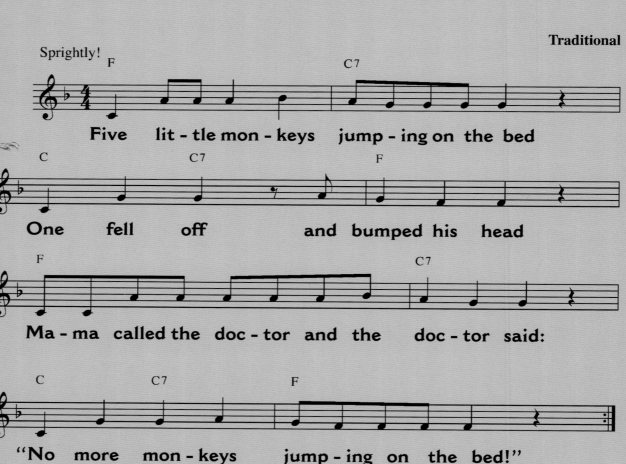

Five lit - tle mon - keys jump - ing on the bed

One fell off and bumped his head

Ma - ma called the doc - tor and the doc - tor said:

"No more mon - keys jump - ing on the bed!"